rochelle ratner
A BIRTHDAY OF WATERS

ACKNOWLEDGEMENTS:

The Nation, Sumac,
The North American Review,
Shenandoah, Antaeus,
The New York Quarterly,
Red Clay Reader,
The World, Cloud Marauder,

Abraxas,
Telephone, Toothpaste,
New York Times
The Ant's Forefoot
Minnesota Review
Cafe Solo

Rochelle Ratner

A BIRTHDAY OF WATERS

Neil Greenberg

drawings

new rivers press

1971

new rivers press books are distributed in

GREAT BRITAIN by   Philip Spender
                   69 Randolph Avenue
                   London, W 9
                   England

           THE UNITED STATES and elsewhere by
                        Serendipity Books
                        1790 Shattuck Avenue
                        Berkeley, California
                        94709

This book was manufactured in the United States for New Rivers
Press, p.o. box 578, Cathedral Station, New York, New York 10025
in a first edition of 600 copies of which 400 are in paperback, 200
in cloth, with 30 of the latter signed and numbered by the author.

for BESS

CONTENTS

Part I

CONSERVATION

i.

I sculpture my brood with my mouth,
produce a formless foetus,
giving birth to ashes
or a bit of pulp.

By licking, I change the stumps
into arms and legs that clutch me
far too soon.

ii.

They promise that my litter
will come in threes.

iii.

Modest,
we've learned to copulate
back to back.
We wear our genitals backwards,
find it's best to look
the other way.

To conceive
we go eastward toward paradise.
I eat of the tree —
mandagora —
then feed some to him.
When we lap it up
it seduces us
and I can feel life stirring in my womb.

iv.

I throw myself on the ground
and pretend not to breathe.
I roll in red mud like a carpet
so he thinks that I'm covered with blood.

A white bird comes down
and will sit on me.   She supposes I'm dead
or her egg.

PREGNANCY

Then the clock was awkward. And her climb
to the brown sky hardened.
                              Breathing
viewed as a recurrence of the stain, as

the gripping arm
falls over pillows. Later on she found him,

a crumbling of low briars
which his fists struck upon, which seemed
as she pushed forward

to be sinking. At every
blistered tick and frenzied echo:
    the jingling, cold sequins of blood,

tired.

    She learned only that all her children
crawled between a name they had written out.

Her breast, it seemed,
which in this flame he entered,

grew too hot.
And she realized he had planned this:
                              he was dead.

    A blanket
hid them both, having fled

together, as a vine.

ON SLEEPLESS NIGHTS IN THE MIDDLE OF WINTER

We kneel as mother's tears
walk down the aisle.

Their steps are tinted white.

We nod.

They pass.

OVER FOOTPRINTS

1.

In Norway
they strip the ice
from children's hands.

They pick through
the bitter crystals
where a woman drags them
home to understand them,
stuffing her arms
with water.

An uncle
watches the bones
buck outward,
   steam
forms a crackling knife
against his touch.

2.

To stare at coal.   To leap
from heavy boots.   To know
the thrill of tightening
under flesh — how we pluck at
that gravel!

   Just a pebble.
Hold it against your chest
until it ripens,
bloats.
  Press
its fine lips to your stomach,

hear its muscles
      flow
like heated oil.

3.

Her staring.   Staring as if
a father never limped.
Deep welts
in the earth: another cousin.

To dig and dig there,
blunt as fire.   No tossing
dust back at the windstorm,
no bundles of clothes

to hide in.

FOR DAD, ON HIS BIRTHDAY, SEPT. 6, 1970

Cool night tonight
window
open
I sit at the desk
cleared off
pajamas loosened
bones
tired
Facing windows
not the
time
for looking out.

FOR YOUR LOST VIOLIN CASE

That day I brought home the doorbell
it was only because you were telling me
about all the friends I'd been expecting
and how they'd glued themselves to the gate.
You called out their names like a fig tree
until I realized it was only the color green
teasing my nightmares this week.

Don't think that I wasn't grateful.
I gave you all the rings I could fit in my stomach.
I showered you with the gold from my eyelids,
the mint from my teeth.
It was you who said no to the new gifts.
I won't ask again.

Even then the box seemed too heavy.
To forget it I turned on the radio,
switching the dial every fifteen minutes
in the hope of accepting a voice.
I was able to doze during Mozart
but it was you who woke me —
You
walking barefoot across the carpet,
having wandered through my garden alone.

REMNANT

I.

The sense of her lying there calms me:

        a lemon rind
        a stone
        a papier mache doll

     getting set to have a ribbon
     tied in its hair.

I keep my eyes focused on the black velvet
that lines the lid of the coffin.   It keeps
threatening to fall on her, close her again
from my sight.

It's as if she were counting backwards from twelve to one.

   Her breath seems to flow
   like the water in a frozen stream.

    Beneath the ice are tiny fossils,
    held in place by the fins
    that brush against them   back and forth.
The trout can swim briskly in water,
alone with the waiting surface of the snow.
                His colors shine frantically,
                   frantically

     my gift.

At night there are stars in the meadow.

   I watch their points swivel, take aim.

Tonight I pick one star
to call my own.   It is not
the brightest   nor is it dull.   It is
                    an average star on an average
                    night.

I pretend to be a grasshopper lost in the field.   My small body
            hunches, crackles

      & then jumps.   I pounce on the weeds,
      on the shadows, on all
      that moves or threatens me with life.

                    Everything dark bends beneath me.
                    I rise
                        & I rise.

      In the grass I am proud
      of my body, its simple lines   Everything
                    seems so calm here.   All is well.

We travel.
We bounce back and forth across cities
                like popping men.

      We crouch in our separate boxes, covered with stars.
      When we wake the music shimmies

      & we bob round.

I think of the black-leaved flower
she wears on her dress.   Its odor fills the room
like broken glass, as if death were hurried, prodded,
propped up on rags.

Here there are too many farmers, too many
lonely men who wish to farm.

The thick topsoil
weighs down their hands
with its fraudulent green.

I sprawl on the velvet
                    (sheltered)
    my head in her lap.

    Her fingers are chilling,
    remorseful.   I press against them,
    a tightrope.

A body grown thin.

Her eyes are like crickets in daylight.

    They dive meekly
    in her skull
    & won't peer out.
                    I hunt for them,
                        awkward,
                            escaping,
            curled into balls of themselves,
                        a borrowed cat.

23

Their haunted wings razor my elbows,
demented guide.

I feel her ghost at play in the woods
where the coon left a path.
                              I become that ghost,
                              that whiteness
                              becomes my shield.
              I flap across mourners.
              delighted.   I am best.
              I am first child.

I am bonded nest in her stomach.   I pound and I plea.

I tell her there were others, but I lie.

                              II.

In my rage I am given a Monday.

A candle burns above her
& drips on her chest.   Its wax forms shapes
                                        forms children
                                        forms a truce.

    It tickles her compact smile
    & she laughs just for me.

I can feel her beckoning toward me
              & almost leave.   But her
              shrouded breasts stop me.   Wait.
                              You begin too soon.   You
                    must be patient.   A sea.

A white bird
sheds its feathers
on the beach.
　　As the wind rises,
　　sand builds in tiny drifts
　　about their guise.
It seems to cradle them,
　　　　　　softly.

Under the waves there are flowers.　Treacherous vines.

Their stems tear across my feet & my ankles grow weak.
They chain me; I cannot leave to meet
the rising tide.

　　In the tents of shepherds
　　she is a sheep.　I
let her skip over the hills
or run wild in the field.

Out of charity I cling to her,
permit her to enter my fruit
so I waken in fear.

She catches birds in her absence,
　　tosses them, sweet on her tongue.
Her shadow is a blurry lantern, resembling hate.
Her heard bones defer me,　　　　　explode.
　　　　　Like air,
　　　　　I am carried across her —

　　a gangster.
　　a wife.

A plane voids the distance between us.

She calls to the Jew
like a savior,

draws a fiddle
from his ashen hair.

We strike up a dance in the darkness, vipers of smoke.

Wasps curl about her face,
swinging in tiny clusters
on the pulse of her breath.
Their glass bodies flutter upward,
          rusting in explanations,
          desperate in groves.

She is a youngster.   Simple.
An embryo trapped.

Day after day I accept her,
                    a gentle return.

She is a paranoid archway,
     an axis of walls,
     a meadow of amulets tied in their primitive myths.

She coils around rivers:
          an owl's shift, birth of prey.   With the abbots
          she wakens, forces the moon to her side
     & is open in love.   I make of her a lampshade,

     naked child.

A nail twists loose from the coffin,
is placed on the blue-flowered river:

           caraway eye.   I grapple,
           emersed in her nectar,
           in love with her god.

I ride on her face like a fire,
hang myself from her palate,
as if a blank snake.

My feet are bare and ordered;
my shoes have been strained.
I fall on my hands as a valley does, crossing the stones.

Part II

Part II

THE HELL DOLL

I.

The pregnant bird
turned loose
in female sky . . .

one wing flapping, turning shyly,
persuasively over the next, steady
falling
tumbling
twisting the clouds into meanings,
into speech. It was
like his hands, now, at the table,
shoveling in and out of themselves
until he can no longer
stand the pressure of her breath.

He sits beside her, an aborted stick.
This was how houses were built, perhaps —
the bricks there so long that they were fixtures,
other things
being forced to take shape around them,
give form to the dirt.

And she—
it was she who had placed him there,
opened the cage to give him his freedom,
give him his hell. He regretted
he'd not met her sooner, not been her wife.
Perhaps the child in himself would be her son.

II.

Inside the duck's beak there is freedom.

On the day of his birth
he bears his second child.
She tears at his womb, arms
groping blindly forth
like a stone in the water.   They almost touch.

A clown who is also a juggler;
his hands pound the wood —
the womb splits, a shattered mirror.

Shapes ridicule themselves like a portrait,
the colors flaring, unnamed.
Two men cannot meet in the darkness.

III.

She is a lute-girl
beckoned to play for him.
She crouches on the narrow floor,
on a blanket perhaps.
Her thin arms
reach tenderly across the strings,
as across his chest.
She would sit there hour on hour,
playing one tune so softly
it seemed she could fly.

Entering the room,
a man might remark on her beauty,
her destined repose.   His breath
might flutter slightly
as her voice pierced him, steady.

From her mother's arms
she'd learned music,
the gentle rhythm of her heartbeats,

her lips swaying back and forth,
enclosing his.

A man might call them lovers, nothing more.

IV.

Her body is a long dark lake
flowing into itself.
He watches always from a distance,
a ship approaching a meadow in the fog.
As day brightens,
he begins to notice tall grass
he mistook for water.

He thinks himself the echo approaching storm.
He will protect her,
cover her,
press her skin against his own,
thus changing places.

It is in much this manner
that he will approach his birth
from the other side.
He will watch his stomach swell
into her being, feel his muscles
tighten, the skin stiff,
long unused.

V.

The Roman emperors were given
shields to be held at their waists.
The bulging metal before them,
they fought for their lives.
In later days

engravings
were printed on gold —
pictures of cavalry,
duels,
scenes that said 'man'.

He is his private boyhood.
His body sprawls on a bed
in darkest night, alone, itself,
with no one
to term it male.
The sound of his blood travels
through him like a battle,
safe, unshod.

VI.

He had seen his mother
naked in the tub.
Her giant breasts hung down, much like his own.

VII.

She is given to picking berries.
She holds them in her hands
and lets them fall.
The tin balls stay
like a man in her throat.
Their soft juice becomes her mother,
tender lips
that have been stolen from his arms.

VIII.

Who
has created the idol?

Who has made the plastic doll?
In the Catholic church a man is the vision of God.

Her flesh is warmed by the fire.
As wax melts it takes on new forms,
becomes a guest.
He would press it against his stomach,
molding it
as she had molded him.
And thus they would worship together, she alone.

BURYING CABBAGE

There are cities where evening is welcome.
Skipping back and forth between the flowers,
a bird seems to turn from your glance.
Windows dispose of their curtains
the way a shadow is growing larger with the breeze.
His head nods.   His hand waves.
Bandages.
White sails are torn by the distance.
The dust leads to trees.

HANDS

You're dirty
It's nothing but greed
I've been patient
I've let you pick my nose
I've bandaged your scabs

You complain of the cold
That does it!
I've decided on mittens
We're finished
I'll soak you in water.

COMBINGS

All things and myself, an old woman
White birds and a child.
Words stinging across empty clotheslines —
It's not for the sea that he saved me,
not for the waves.

I speak to him:
steam and our bodies,
like trains in an emerald of sleep.
It was dark and the feet in the traffic,
the pawmarks I change into iron —
The iron abounds.

EVE

I have woken up with the turtle.
His short claws dig at me like diamonds
and cannot be lost.
He is my stolen gold wristwatch;
I am his heart.

No, I am not the intruder —
    I slept with him
    Dreamt with him
    Walked with him
Waited in sand.

THE LAST BUFFALO

The last buffalo
follows you up the staircase.
He thinks the house
the rooms   the walls
are playmates in a game of skipping ropes.

In the cellar, Brueghel's landscapes
gather crowds.   A six-gun shoots an Indian
who's running from the stream.

Lights dim as naked bodies
brush against the ending of a voice.
Our flesh slides under mirrors, over dust.
The cow's breath
is a child at the twisted lute.

THE TEETH OF THE WALRUS

In the teeth of the walrus,
a drunkard.   The sun has
its own strange magic,
headed home.   And yet she
meets him in the pathway —
        running,
                leaping forward,
                jumping down.

Her lips
fasten onto the air
as she grips his fur.   She
calls him by her name,
        and she replies.

RAIN

1.

We weren't afraid of the marigolds, clinging like
breasts to a tree. There are hurricanes now. And they
know us. Our shadows grow damp.

2.

A rat hears his name in the wind and he wakens
to wait. His eyes are the deep veins of milkweed;
his headache is proud. He might have stored chestnuts
for winter, shedding black gills like the sea,
But they told him the rain would bear children.
They told him. He's waiting to hear.

3.

She enters the house like a calendar, anxious as night.
It was dark. We were sleeping. We slept there.
We slept there and woke to the stillness
of water. The stillness of fish.

ACADEMICS

God is eating the sun.
A tasty lemon rind
falls to the floor of the castle.
Mice glance at you quickly.
There's clouds.

THE WINDOWS

Opened
like greeting cards, yet
colorful, a thin arm
on my shoulder, chapping
lips at my side, my
glance a distinction:
she is the father, she,
she is, herself.   I hold
her arm up to the light
with a piercing, like
a heavy weight
or stones rolled from the steps
or stones found in the grass
hidden from themselves between our watching.
It seems I have given her thread.

I see sweaters.   I contain
all the memories
and the fanatic lights of the water.
Again the glow of a rifle
hurts my ears.   A collar of white birds
flies over us, flying in twos.

AT THE BOLES OF MY ARMS

> *"It was the rise of flowering plants*
> *that provided the energy to change the*
> *nature of the living world.   Their*
> *appearance parallels in quite a sur-*
> *prising manner the rise of birds and*
> *mammals."*
>
>   *— Loren Eisely*
>   *The Immense Journey*

At first I cling to swamps,
as is my need. My gorged
organs demand it be damp.
His sperm
wriggles up through the waves
till it pecks at my cells.

I remain in the background, silent,
because I have not yet thought
to use the wiles of insects,
spread word of my sex.
I sow my own seed
or receive the seeds of others
by a pact made with wind.

I grow a child in my shadow,
at last independent of streams.
He is packed in a little box
which I've stuffed full of food.
Wafted upward,
he journeys on gusts
or forms hooks and clings to a bear's
or rabbit's hide.

My vision changes daily,
like the moon.
I am pale, unearthly,
intended to lure moths
in the evening light,
or I take the shape of a spider
to attract him.

THE POTATO

The potato is on the dishrack
The washable pyrex frypan is in the closet
The dog is outside

*

The potato is being cut into slices
The knife moves leisurely from right to left,
enhanced by the efforts of sunlight
The last slice appears somewhat different

*

The potato is baked in a wine sauce
The child stares at it angrily,
stuffing his mouth with the warm flesh of a cow

The potato grows cold, giving off a faint gold light
The candles are still in their boxes

The child takes down one box, opens it,
and twists the wax rhythmically thru his fingers
He seems to be very contented

*

The potato is in a jar on the windowsill
You have been watering it faithfully every day

On warm days the window is open
Sparrows perch on the rim of the jar,
taking proud sips from the water
Some stay there longer than others.

GETTING THERE

The street was dark as worn tires
and you had your lunch —
blue veins, leaves and butterflies
all in a brown paper bag.
My thighs are accepted now.
Thank you.

The hinting of frogs.

At last we're amending the oranges,
pears not yet ripe.
Row, row   And fish know the answers.
We differ from wind.

DRESS REHEARSAL

I love you like wood and you laugh
with high birds I can't see.
White flat ducks wake the morning to leaves
that have slanted from night.

Talk...talk...I hear noises —
It's only the fish that are flying now,
bodies and words.

Borrowed sunlight is crossing our sleep
like a child in the woods.
It's cold and then warm in the haloes,
the dark strung together like travel.

Time was geology then.
It was summer.   We always had friends.

PASSION IN BROOKLYN

This is the dawn of blue fishes,
fog and cigar smoke
The river is young, wearing underwear
They stare at each other
Those walls

Feathers, worms, streams of fire
The shadows begin here
The sweat   What a cockroach does
Walk

Open windows
The clouds, small and lead
And they're playing now
Boats on the shore

Truer roses

The waves seeming friendly
Bark   Bark
And the pebbles   The grass
It was tennis   Deep, creepy
Your hair in the bathtub

The sewer
The name of the sun.

MARRIAGE

The elevator pushes us off and we wander about.
A strange man walks up behind you and taps your shoulder
"not too close to the edge" he cautions,
but you're too busy walking to hear him.   You take
a few more steps and the air offers vodka martinis.
The neon swoops down and blue jays are pausing to sip from them,
tilting the olives before you have time to accept.

THE BLACK SMOKE

The black smoke rising out there
like paws on a jungle-jim,
I want to see a bird's wing hiding them
I want to
I want to see a bird,
a jumble of tiny white mites
kissing it,
ants can make love to it. . .

Morning;
the thought of Japan and the thought of
Jamaica,
the thought stays,
the wings fondling me,
the seed fell when the wind paused
about when I watched it
about when my mother grew proud
of my thoughts and my birthday but
she couldn't have known how
I spoke to my priest to my
teacher spoke to my daughter
my lamp not always but
then the black smoke
the grey smoke
the smoke curving over us
wait, what a tribute to flowers,
the bricks stand beside the water-tanks
the hand shakes
the puppies grow rancid just huddled there
a fellow in orange walks up to you,
steadies your arm.

POEM BEGINNING 'A WARM NIGHT'

A warm night / a warm week
counting from star
                    to star
                            to star,
calling them mirrors or only reflectors —
these shapes in the dense
or spayed forests.
                    We say that the fox
does not reason; even his fur stirs in tribute.
He knows to lead the dogs,
but not as we do.
When eggs fry it's better to hide
in the brush near a narrow slope;
better than running, or scheming,
less tiring
to be high on a neck he could watch them,
the black spots and claws.

   Five trees,
tall ones sensing twenty hammers —
even now we have recalled
the thrill of adding.   Even as rain
on the leaves removes our shadows
or a fork is lifted.

                    So the river, guest,
is behind you.   And then fifty icings
of weed.   One would think to drink with you,
wander like you on the ledges.

ACTAEON

A weed is growing in the meadow,
cold rain, beige, orange weed,
infusing and then seeing from the clocks,
coming near us like Bach on a tongue.

At last it finds the huge beast's chow,
innocent shovels fording slowly in the air.
You feel warm about what we are losing
by turning close to each other, threading
the dust.
        Slipping through bays,
when the shadows of frost appear wiry
and more intimate than these flowers,
continually calling each other
instead of casually discovering them
next to you, brown and untruthful.

THE GODDESS IN SUMMER

1.

The abyss of her jaw flutters wildly.
Water drips from the roof of her mouth
and her throat has a gurgle —
hollow, and frightening to see.

A greenness juts out from her ribs
like a huge plant, without life.

2.

Naked fish and insects
flow through her chest.
They dart between her bones
or construct tubes of sand to house them
so that they are safe.

It is always damp and cool here;
often a bear or fox
will be discovered sleeping
and out of the sun.

3.

It grows cooler.

Perhaps her lips are closed now,
trapping light.

Tiny white creatures
in water
have no eyes.

They cluster in lagoons
or silt-bottomed pools
where leaf
and twig fragments give
a sort of warmth.

4.

Her legs are filled with rapids,
tense and thin.
You crawl along them
up and away from the stream,
almost lifeless yourself.

At times she seems dry
but tender —
you scatter no dust.

Along her flesh
there are scallop-like markings
which tell you her age.

5.

Deep shafts
form in her bones now.
The water splashes
clearly
against the clear sand.

She carries no plants here,
no sex.

As you move on
the passage grows larger
and you can stand up.

6.

Her weak muscles
are almost collapsing.
Blood runs down the sides of her body
And supplies a natural basin
in the bones.
A fine black coating
covers the air at the edge.

This is an oasis of foliage.
It washes in
during spring floodings
by way of her hands.

7.

As you round her breasts
nearing your exit,
you are met by an eerie blue light.

Getting closer,
you see it's your eyes
that are shadowed in hers.

Small webs are knit in her cheekbones
and it seems that pale brown crickets
are perched on her lips.
They are forced to leave her when hungry,
but only on blunt, humid nights.

Part III

THE CURSE OF BRIGHT WATERS

I.

A bitch is the age of the landscape.
She is the same age as that granite,
that shit she walks upon.
The trees reach out at her like brothers,
accusing fingers sticky in her gut.
They taunt,
they yearn to jeer at her,
ape her steps along the narrow ridge.
The sea on one side,
father's smile below.

It is always beginning winter
in seaside resorts.
It is its own fear handed over —
a whitened sheet,
a rock-bed,
a towering light that echoes
round and round.
She would take charge of the lighthouse,
guide the ships in circles
toward their homes.
And she would speak of this
that all might know.

This is no place for children.
Let their mothers beckon all in pain,
but no —
the rocks shall never shed a tear.
So keep son or daughter hidden;
adopt him,
take him home,

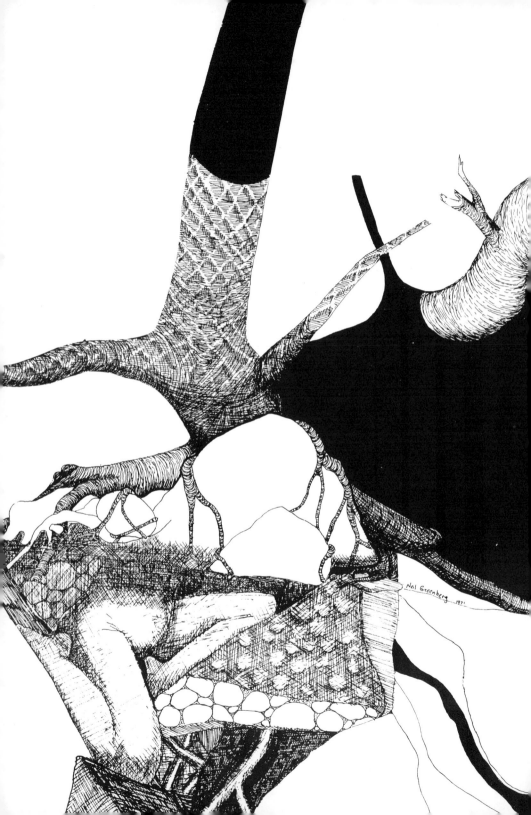

and call him yours.
Do not let him wander past his voice.

. . . . .
If she seeks resurrection in wind,
she becomes the wind.
The land is her silent bed-mate,
always there on waking,
there to wake.
She would bleed, but never stain it,
give birth,
but never ask to name the child.

So it is one-third earth
and one-third love;
she who views it adds the other third.
The rocks,
damp now with tears,
would be dry in a day or two.
It seldom takes longer
than that to understand.

. . . . .
The sea is a mistress in daylight,
a father at night.
Its beastly hands push forward,
attacking her dreams.
Its heavy breath pounds
against the walls of her private room,
almost knocking them down.
It even contains its own laughter,
a tuning-fork pinched,
tossed aside.

. . . . .
She had seen her parents
buried in the soil.

She had seen her god, a child,
slide down the hill.
In the air behind her eyes
she had cried for their deaths.

Men had dug canals in stagnant land.
Perhaps someday water would flow here,
give to this village
what her fathers stole.
Deer would sip as they sipped
from a river, tricked by man.
Her eyes seemed to clench
at the thought of it —
she would grow drunk on her sweat;
she would not drink!
The fate of the deer
like the fate of the buffalo —
so would surely be the fate of man.
A species only lives
to become extinct.

. . . . .
Fossils,
bones in museums,
a skull for the prize.
She cradled herself like
a sewer in his arms.
And he would sing to her —
sing to her like the hiss
of flowing mud.
City after city built on land.
Building after building
formed of clay.

The pollution of water and air.
The polluted heart.
How many years the wasted words

had been building up.
The dam of her tongue overflowed,
and she was glad.
Like a beaver her tail was limp,
alone,
afraid.
She had built her life
on the wreckage of her voice.

. . . . .

The land gives birth two times —
once to a son
and once to a daughter.
The oldest child dies soon
and becomes her hymn.
Let the trees become a steeple,
the mountain a dome;
let the sound of footsteps
be a prayer.
Yisgadal v'yiskadash sh'mei raba . . .
mourners rise.

II.

All around me grows to giant height.
I will not bear the son,
but carve the branch.
I perch on the oak tree's limb,
both god and child.
I become the bird in passing,
marble-footed, clothed.
I bear the message
from a distant hill.
My flight is a circle
as my steps are not.

A red fox barks in the lonely night.

This is the call of winter —
I must leave. I must
fly south to find my mate.
Mountain will couple with mountain —
I lie between.

. . . . .

A dog runs across the beach —
a large brown dog.
It is the self that's mirrored
in the waves —
the running self.
I imagine myself as he is,
unknown to the land.
In the final stage of sleep
my bones grow frail;
they crack like painted clay,
they wilt like brick.
In the building of my mind
the sky is calm.

A cloud will hide the bird,
will hide my face:
man's steam,
it is my guardian,
my mirage, my private lake.
I close on myself like a furnace
atop a roof. Fly low, child.
Oh, fly low!

. . . . .

I wear a white satin sweatshirt
and diamond shoes.
The sun is my father:
father-sun.
I walk in the busied city,
a vacant road within the skidding car.

His thin penis shrinks at my side
like the neck of a tree.
I might have borrowed lead from him,
fired real bullets at clay.

. . . . .

I accept my body only when swimming nude.
I drink from the river
as I would have him drink;
I hand my son
what water's handed me.
The debris cast up in the night
will be my sin.   The waves
grow dim with my swimming here,
grow dark with the weight of my arms.

In the wind I will murder my children.
I will tear out their stomachs
like clam shells,
ride their muscles like a leash
into second death.
I will be reborn in the mountain's hip.

. . . . .

I have known no fear to chain my birth.
I escape from the land's reply
and am buried at sea.
The prow of a boat glides across me,
I sink and I rise.
I am the taste of dead water,
the scent of struck land.
All who cross must offer refuge to my soul.

I am hanged man, hanged woman —
the dart game played alone
from the mountain's peak.
I spin quickly beneath a feather

and then return.
Inside my jaws are forests unprepared.

. . . . .

I will walk along the river made by man.
I will accept his mockery,
his hate.
I will learn chants to call forth dream,
to call forth night.
I will be the speaking field
that calls the plow.

I will be the arm raised to god
that brings forth rain.
As boat nudges boat in water,
so I reach.
It is the snake that rides here,
curls,
recoils.

I rejoice that the trees have shadows.
In their arc I make repentance,
confess to all the evils
of barren fields.
I draw the cross in soil
that the wind may grow damp,
that the water may have a pathway
from its source.
— Are my bones not that source?
No, they are not.
I carry my own shadow as I walk.

STRESSES

I.

At last her thin stomach
has its glass eyes no longer
for comfort.

Before the mirrors are hidden
they pierce the black bricks into threes.
A naked bird is limping in its cage.

At one time

the tray of food that had despised her,
and her green sweater, and her hairpins
clamped in song.

II.

I can hear the ragged fieldmouse
in the south

dry sweatshirt

shirking from the clouds of which I tell him.

III.

Within this creased autumn thunder
the sky is a plant

and the head of a wren
lashes back.

BROOKLYN HEIGHTS — A GAME, A RIVER

i.

A preacher is shrinking around me.
From his half of the wall I am hidden,
as I would choose.
Low voices are bypassed beneath me,
trains on the cognizant track.
I ride there, a passenger,
sculpture,
my eyes against glass.

The landscape folds into me,
touches me,
gives me its hand.
The duplicate mountains surround me;
as I climb I count, but don't let on.

ii.

The cat's ear floats off
and she runs to it,
chases a buried string across the floor.

I take refuge in the sea,
a sunken raft.
My body is bounced through his water
and tossed against rocks like an airplane,
his robot with wings.
At the cliff's chest I am nibbling politely,
branding my tongue with a jewel.

CHINA: CIRCA 820 A.D.

In brutish winter
what there is to love
covers the hills
with a white dawn
On a bank
where bamboos
sprouted
darkened torches
welcome a new kinsman
damped
by a black flag
of cloud

To the left and right
in the air
the sunlight thins
the view
empties

Back
from a walk
he lies
under the front eaves
their only lodger,
a toadstool
which dies
in a morning
High in the sky
one mirror rises
crumbling
like fresh-hoed soil

The pulley creaks
at the well,

curly
like ancient script,
neatly composed
like a portrait
By the green shores
are a few torn
sails with
nothing
but the name
of a drifter.

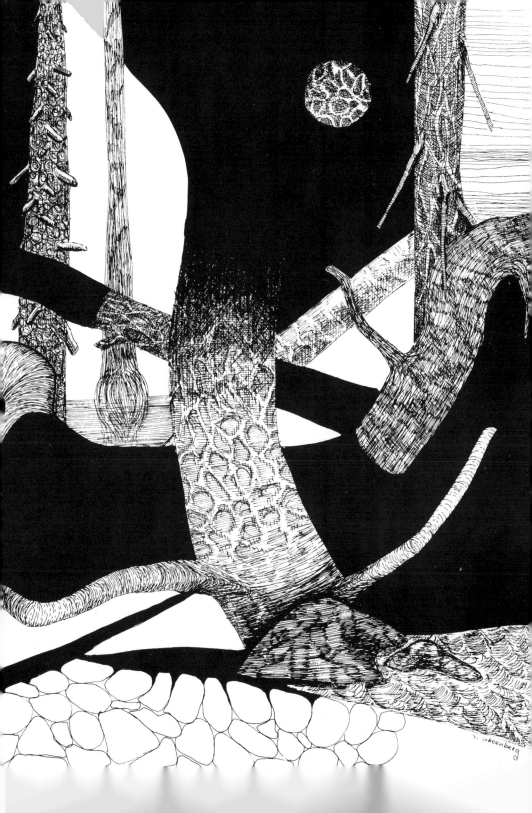

THE GEESE PURRING

The geese purring, near sleep, before turning their heads —

You begin, a threat to the distance.
But not eyes, not leaves, not windmills
will hinder your pattern,
your mountain.
You contain the remembrance of woman
as stars contain night.
              The sky
is a ghost of its very thunder,
where the flight of the homing-bird
howls
in silence —
the stillness, no less still than you.

Having approached you quickly,
from behind,
the clouds have won, their fur stiffens.

The black discs press their thighs
against your breast,
whether you stir or are resting.

No takers.
Night after night the wings flicker,
grow heavy and fade, without calling.
Mask. Willow not pregnant nor warm
in the grass where you hide.
You wake here, a casual flower

observing no change

but with the next seed beating at your lips,
desperate for sound, enclosing sound.

To be a woman's necklace

clasping, held onto
by secret strings, in the evening,
when the flight is of hands and thoughts, preparing.

WIZARDS

1.

   The sky's arch and limp
Wizards are in conference there on chimneys
Wizards are red brick

   Wings the near-sighted
wings to brush their glasses when the air fogs and steam
spurts trees flail the night-breeding streetsigns
gasp in pain

   Encased as a jewel
   son who touches
cars the city restless in its coffin

   Above them the lights.

2.

   What a path
your gold-tinted footsteps
feel free to turn into

         (the wind did not grow looser
         that the grey vines sprouted)
And then you quickly spin to look behind you
You hope to spot an eye that will choose
      one roof from the rest and flash rings
         Your circling horse!

   The wizards draw close to you
In the morning the cloudburst relies on you
Cars stop to let you cross
         and you walk slowly

Slow prince no one wakens.

SPRING RECESS

I.

She sleeps hearing puddles.
The branch of an oak is not seen in this storm.
Leaves, as they fly backwards, feel
the flames reaching down.
The grey nuts drift to a hollow stalk.

Like a cloudburst filling green balloons,
feel the light falling off you.
    The glass we breathe away from
is refracted in our hands.

Pebbles burst at the windmill;
a tulip combs its eyes into the mirror.
We give her plums but they turn to raisins,
flicking shadows we no longer step on.
The statues are wet, like the asphalt.

II.

Red trees.
The clapping sticks of familiar reappraisal
are stolen from magnitude
and reflected in the shy lake
Motionless phonetic parents
sway back and forth on the ground.

The farmhouse defines what is vision
as women walk along the slow road,
each cloud returned to the issuing skyline
Pink to green to silver
               and then back

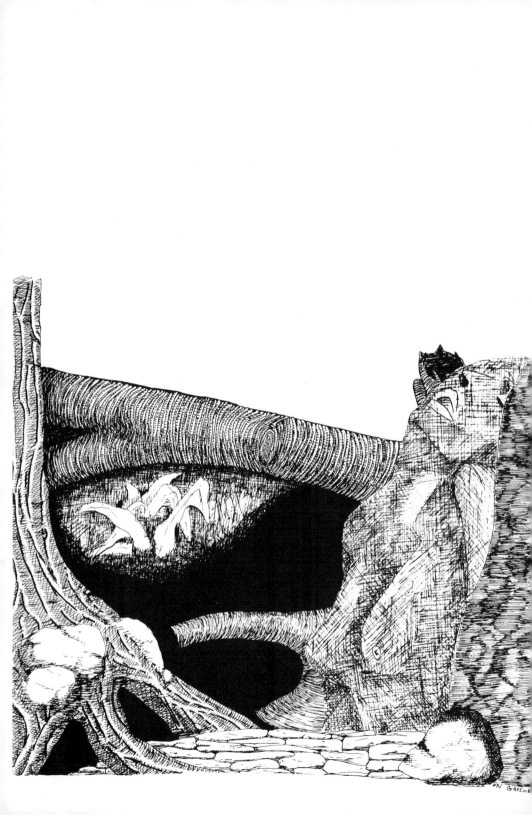

The yellow brush remains blameless
A wheel turns with
and not against your breath.

III.

You find so many tall bushes along the mountains
Voices of living valleys appear in the distance
Shadows almost fold with the warm blankets
Large plants appearing in the moon
Millions of sentimental wings hiding grass or tall weeds . . .
The landscape returns to where you dreamt it
There are some first leaves with a tint of completed hues
There are some imaginitively-lifted sundials
Now and then in the morning a small cat cries and his image can be
                                        seen in the east

Yesterday I sank a steamship to the bottom of the sea
Still the same waves of tired gulls
The Egyptian mistress uncovers some humming-birds
Everyone is wearing green make-up
We go up to the top of the lighthouse
For us it's the first remembrance of ships lost in storms.

The temperature changes
Our attire is childish skirts and a white lace blouse
Secrets are important for the baggage we have hidden
In the evening we simply put aprons over our skirts
Skiffs and kayaks brush us with their sails.

IV.

Wagons under streetlights carry sweaters held to skin;
this evening there will be a quarter moon.
In the darkness,
in the bronze that's drifting toward us

the petals of a weed have distant thoughts.

The stranger turns to speak to us
with the frailness of his breathing reaching out
on the asphalt, seeming cousinly and warm.
A sea laps up the many pebbles
of beaches while a wing folds in the clouds.

Someone has been pausing at the window —
it is a feeling we have always known . . .
while we listen you press your hands against the humming
as the seed against the lisping soil.

V.

Blue kite using the orange sky
and as usual the clouds are too strong for sunlight
so if the string falls
jackets unbutton and wait for us.
You are walking slowly now
Trucks toss some hot foam into my fingers
where I can feel the cool waters.

The wind hunching into my sight
low in these valleys
like a farmer.
Trucks rolled forward
like a road near a thunderstorm
and your leaves mounted to the clouds
as if they were postcards withered by dust.

I don't really know about fishing-boats.
Once I sat on a bicycle

far away from the wheels of a river
and was never awakened.
Leaves brushed against me and continued on
I was happy then but now
a branch has fallen across the careful string.

VI.

A mask of cushions in the April noon
I stood alone
And heard the sun fall across the courtyard
Like a broken oboe.
Close by me the windows flowed northward
With cold orange lips like a swan.

Like a chameleon my eyes have opened
In fragrant marsh
And shuffling through my footsteps
Purple leaves beat and cling.

The pine needle
Falls from my back like a storm cloud
Gathers dampness to its ridges
And the burnt arms
Drift beneath it.

VII.

This wind cannot keep blowing,
it ceases —
        A unison.

The thick chest of a river
recoils in my path. I wait, I
notice the quick lights of memories

moving north.   Complacency troubles the shore.

When the sun sets I sail to the tropics.
All the natives in their gay skirts,
all the husbands rejecting deadlines
in my eyes.   If only there were not this resentment
that the waves walk before us.

I wait, my mouth
waters itself at the thinking.
Tomorrow the women travel from their homes.
The door of my cabin is rocking —
A careful shape, a leaf, moves across the sea.

VIII.
Faces
eyes untouched
meticulous zircons cold now
a calm feather on a calm leaf
sees us,
    I hear a stone

I hear a corner of the river
a plant stroking air

Laughing, I hear
a houseboat and the children
pressing back, I

hear pebbles on their fingers
the lips of berries fall
the clasp of water nourishing.

IX.

That the woman

grey as half open windows
should pause by the river this evening
and unfold her necklace
like the breeze reluctant
above a stone no bird has injured.
an orange stone possibly.

The most tender birthday
begins fairly close to a forest . . .
excited lobsters move on cardboard walls.
She would curl like a seagull in rain-clouds
but she hasn't been told about wetness.
her hands bend in steam.

Once again I sit on a tree stump
allowing moss to make me thirsty until
like a spider I thrust these pebbles
into the snow of consistency.
Wood becomes black near the sand dunes.

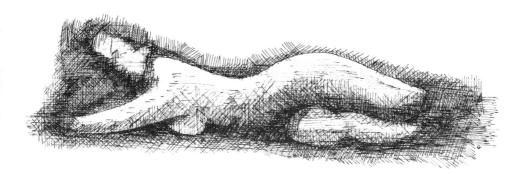